Weekend at Muskrat Lake

by NICKI WEISS

GREENWILLOW BOOKS, NEW YORK

10 9 8 7 6 5 4 3 2 1

Library of Congress Cataloging in Publication Data
Weiss, Nicki.   Weekend at Muskrat Lake.
Summary: Pearl and her family spend a weekend at
a lake and enjoy many activities including swimming,
blueberry picking, and fishing.   [1. Lakes—Fiction.
2. Country life—Fiction. 3. Family life—Fiction]
I. Title.   PZ7.W448145We 1984   [E]   83-20789
ISBN 0-688-03767-4   ISBN 0-688-03768-2 (lib. bdg.)

Swimming

"Don't let go, Mama," Pearl said.

Pearl was learning how to swim, and Mama held on to her as they headed back to the shore.

"I won't, dear," said Mama, "not until you're ready."

Pearl's feet touched the lake's bottom, and she started to walk the rest of the way.

"It's so squishy here," she said.

"There's clay at the bottom," Mama said. "Some lakes have sandy bottoms and some have clay."

She reached down and took a handful. "I bet we could make things out of this," she said.

Pearl reached down and took a handful, too.

Pear learns how to swim
- Trust her mom to hold her

Some lakes have
sand or clay @ the bottom.

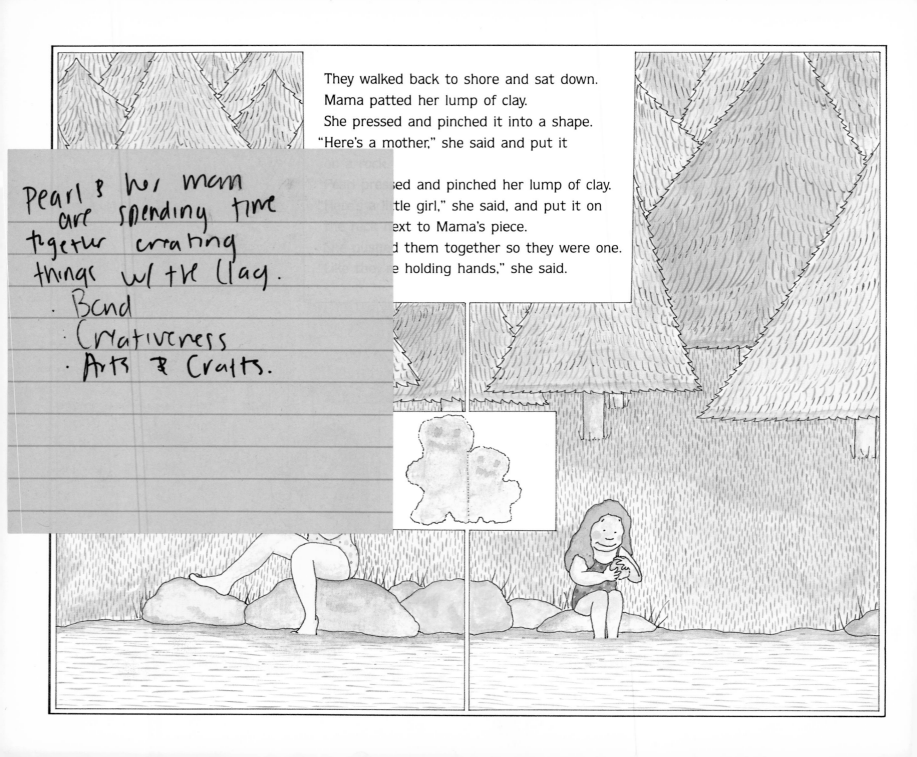

They walked back to shore and sat down.
Mama patted her lump of clay.
She pressed and pinched it into a shape.
"Here's a mother," she said and put it

...sed and pinched her lump of clay.
...tle girl," she said, and put it on
...ext to Mama's piece.
...d them together so they were one.
...e holding hands," she said.

Then they went into the water and got more clay.
Mama made another little figure.
"And here is the little girl's big sister," she said, placing it
on another rock.
"Here's the daddy," said Pearl, and it was put on a rock, too.
More clay, and more figures.
Soon there was a little clay dog, cat, snake, fish, bear, and
butterfly sitting on the rocks.
"Let's leave them to dry in the sun," Mama said, "while we
take one more swim to the raft and back."

Mama held her arm around Pearl's waist as they paddled toward the raft.
A few feet away from it Pearl said, "I think I can make it there by myself. But stay right next to me, Mama."
Mama let go, and Pearl made her way to the raft.
"I did it!" she said. "I swam by myself!

- Pearl was abu to swim back w/ her mom.
Gained confidence in herself to let go

"It wasn't very far, though," she added as she and Mama climbed onto the raft.

"Just a little bit at a time," Mama said, "and soon you'll be able to do it all by yourself."

They gazed toward the shore and could see the clay figures sitting on the rocks.

"I hope they're dry when we get back," said Pearl, "so we can take them home."

Swimming back, Mama held Pearl until she asked to be let go. "But stay close by, Mama," said Pearl.
And when her feet touched bottom, she said, "I did it again! All by myself."

Then Pearl checked to see if the clay figures were dry.
"I'll take the mother and little girl," she said.
But when she picked them up off the rock, they were
brittle, and the mother and little girl broke apart.
"Oh, look, Mama," Pearl said. "They're not together anymore."

"I can help you put them together," Mama said, "when we get home. A little water should make them stick again."

Pearl carefully held both figures in one hand and put her other hand in Mama's.

"Tomorrow I bet I could go all the way to the raft by myself," she said.

"There's no need to do it all at once," Mama said. "Not until you're ready." —Not go alone.

She squeezed Pearl's hand and they started up the path.

Blueberry Picking

"Slow down," Pearl said to her big sister Rosemary.
"I can't follow you if you walk so fast."
"That's the idea," said Rosemary as they took the path
that ran along the lake.
Then they found the patch of blueberry bushes right
at the edge of the water.
"These three over here are mine," Rosemary said.
"You pick those over there."
Pearl started picking.

"Blueberry muffins don't taste nearly as good as blueberry pie,"
Rosemary said, eating out of the pail.
"I like them," said Pearl.
"Besides," Rosemary said, "you don't need as many blueberries
for muffins as you do for a pie."
She put another handful in her mouth.
"They're too easy to make."

The sun lowered in the sky and the air felt cooler. From the house the girls could hear Mama calling to come home.

"We better get going," Pearl said, "if we want to bake anything."

Rosemary eyed Pearl's pail, full of blueberries. Then she looked into her own half-empty one.

"I thought maybe we'd make a pie together," she said. "If we put yours with mine, we could make the biggest blueberry pie you ever saw."

"No way," said Pearl. "Remember, only one person per pie, Rosemary. And I'm going to make one by myself."

"I thought you wanted to make blueberry muffins," Rosemary said.

"They're too easy," said Pearl, turning toward the path.

"Well, they're not that easy," Rosemary said. "I'm going to make the best blueberry muffins you ever tasted."

She ran past Pearl.

Pearl followed, hugging her heavy pail of blueberries.

Fishing

Tap-tap-tap.

Pearl opened her eyes.

It was still dark out.

"Whoever's going fishing with me better get a move on,"

Papa whispered as he tapped again on the door.

"You getting up?" Pearl asked Rosemary.

Rosemary grunted and pulled the covers over her head.

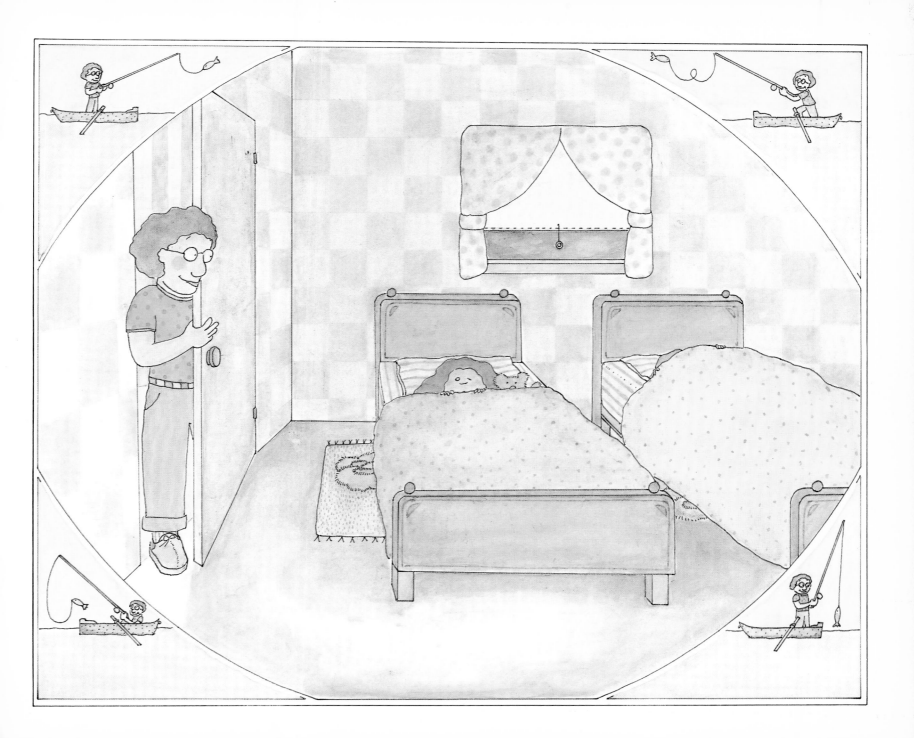

Oatmeal eaten, Papa and Pearl
tiptoed so as not to wake
Mama and Rosemary.
But the floorboards still
squeaked.
"Worms," Papa whispered.
"Can't forget the worms."
Out on the dark porch, Papa
switched on the flashlight and
found his rod.
"You carry the worms," he
whispered. "They're over there."
Pearl reached for a pail by the
door.

Papa aimed the flashlight on
the path.
It was so quiet, all Pearl could
hear were the crickets.
Somewhere an owl hooted.
"Almost time for him to go to
sleep," Papa said.
Then they stepped down the
path, and the gravel crunched
under their feet.

Even before they got to the lake, Pearl could hear the water lapping against the shore.
"You hold the flashlight while I push the boat into the water," Papa said, "and be careful
not to spill the worms."
Crunch crunch. Papa lifted and pulled the boat over the gravel toward the lake.
Whish whish. The boat glided over the tall grass and into the water.
First the rod, then the pail, Papa lifted Pearl into the boat and then climbed in himself.

The boat started drifting.

"Can I row first?" asked Pearl.

"Sure," Papa said.

Clink. One oar dropped into the oarlock.

Clink. Papa put the other one in, too.

Pearl took the middle seat and Papa arranged his gear.

Creak, swoosh. The oarlocks were rusty in the old wooden boat.

Creak, swoosh. The boat moved away from the shore.

Creak, swoosh. Pearl pulled hard on the oars, and Papa lit his pipe.

"This is my favorite time of day," he said.

Creak, swoosh, creak, swoosh.

Pearl rowed until she couldn't anymore, and she switched seats with Papa.

"Watch out for the pail, Papa," she said.

Then for a moment they just sat and listened.

Plop.

Plop plop.

"Hear that?" Papa asked. "Fish."

Creak, swoosh. Papa rowed and the boat moved much faster than when Pearl had rowed.

Creak, swoosh. Pearl thought that Papa's pipe smelled good in the early morning air.

Creak, swoosh. Papa pulled the oars into the boat and said, "I think it's light enough for me to start."

He picked up the fishing rod.

He carefully attached the hook to the line.

"Okay, Pearl," he said. "Pass me the worms."

Pearl wrinkled her nose as she pulled the pail from under the seat.

But as she handed it to Papa, they both stared into it.

"Blueberries?" Papa said. "A pail of blueberries?"

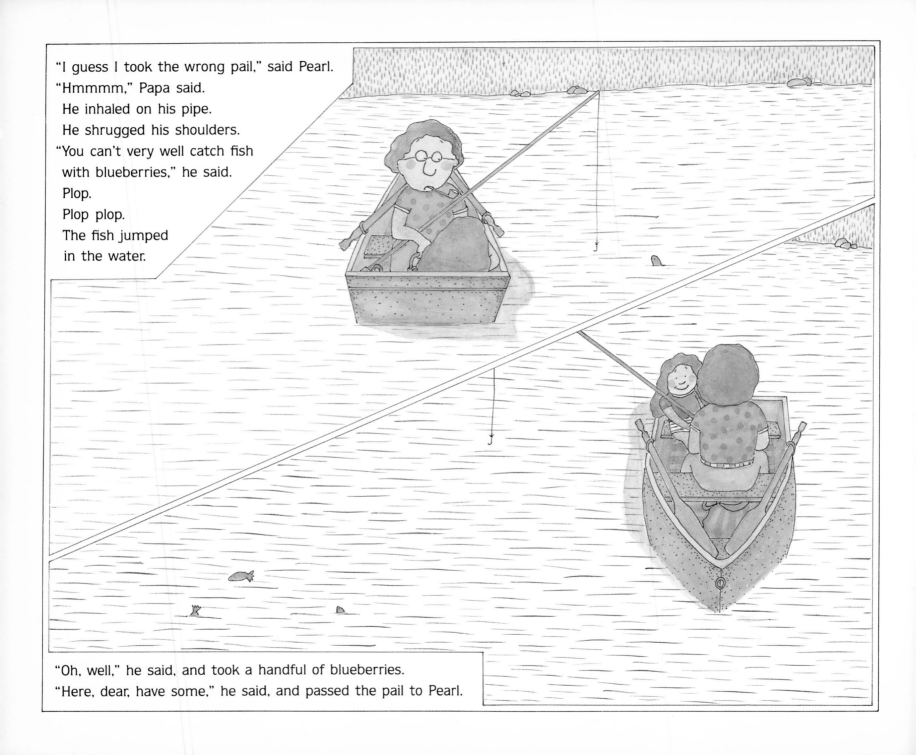

"I guess I took the wrong pail," said Pearl.
"Hmmmm," Papa said.
He inhaled on his pipe.
He shrugged his shoulders.
"You can't very well catch fish
with blueberries," he said.
Plop.
Plop plop.
The fish jumped
in the water.

"Oh, well," he said, and took a handful of blueberries.
"Here, dear, have some," he said, and passed the pail to Pearl.

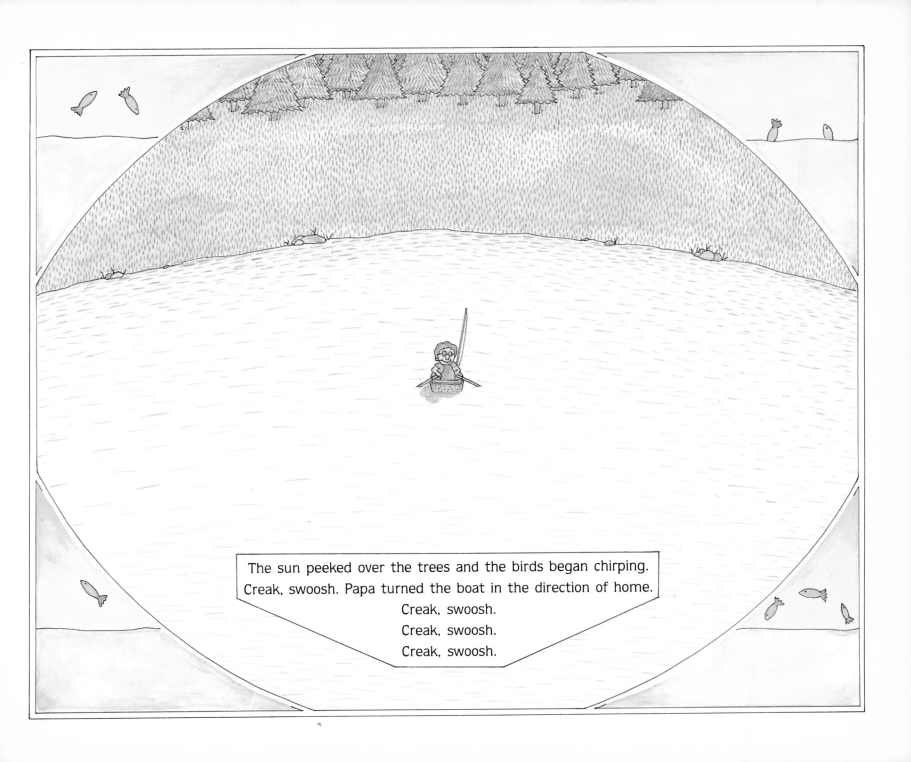

The sun peeked over the trees and the birds began chirping.
Creak, swoosh. Papa turned the boat in the direction of home.
Creak, swoosh.
Creak, swoosh.
Creak, swoosh.

Muskrat Lake

The coals were still glowing in the grill after dinner. Pearl and Rosemary, Mama and Papa stood around it, roasting marshmallows.

"I wonder why they call it Muskrat Lake," Pearl said. "I haven't seen a muskrat since we got here."

"You wouldn't know one if you saw one," said Rosemary, taking a marshmallow out of the bag.

"To tell you the truth," Mama said, "I don't think I've seen a muskrat in all the years we've been coming. If you ask me," she added, "Clay Bottom Lake would be a better name. After all, there's plenty of that around here."

"Maybe muskrats hide because they're scared of people," said Pearl, sticking a marshmallow on the end of her stick.

"Come to think of it," said Papa, "I don't think I've seen one either. If I named the lake I'd call it Trout Lake. After all, there are plenty of them around here, not that I've hooked any lately."

Pearl watched as her marshmallow burned to a crisp.

"Maybe muskrats hide because they're afraid that people are going to catch them," she said.

"That's disgusting," Rosemary said, looking at Pearl's marshmallow. Pearl put it in her mouth.

"Well, I think that Muskrat Lake is a dumb name and they should call it Queen Rosemary Lake," said Rosemary.
"After all, there's only one of me around here."
"Maybe muskrats hide because they think that people make too much noise," said Pearl, and she took
another marshmallow out of the bag.

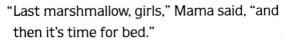

"Last marshmallow, girls," Mama said, "and then it's time for bed."

"I'll get some water to put out the coals," said Papa, and he walked toward the lake. Rosemary and Pearl ate their last marshmallows and Papa came back with a bucket of water.

He sprinkled it over the coals, and they hissed until they were cool.

"Muskrat Lake is an okay name, even if I've never seen one," Pearl said. "I bet they'll come out after we're gone."

"I know why you like muskrats," said Rosemary. "They're little with beady eyes and like to eat, just like you."

She walked up the porch steps and into the house.

Pearl slowly followed.

But just as she was about to go inside,
Pearl thought she heard a noise.
She looked around.
Nothing was there.

The door swung shut behind Pearl.
And in the bushes next to the house, the leaves rustled.
With a scurry of paws, a muskrat ran across the lawn.

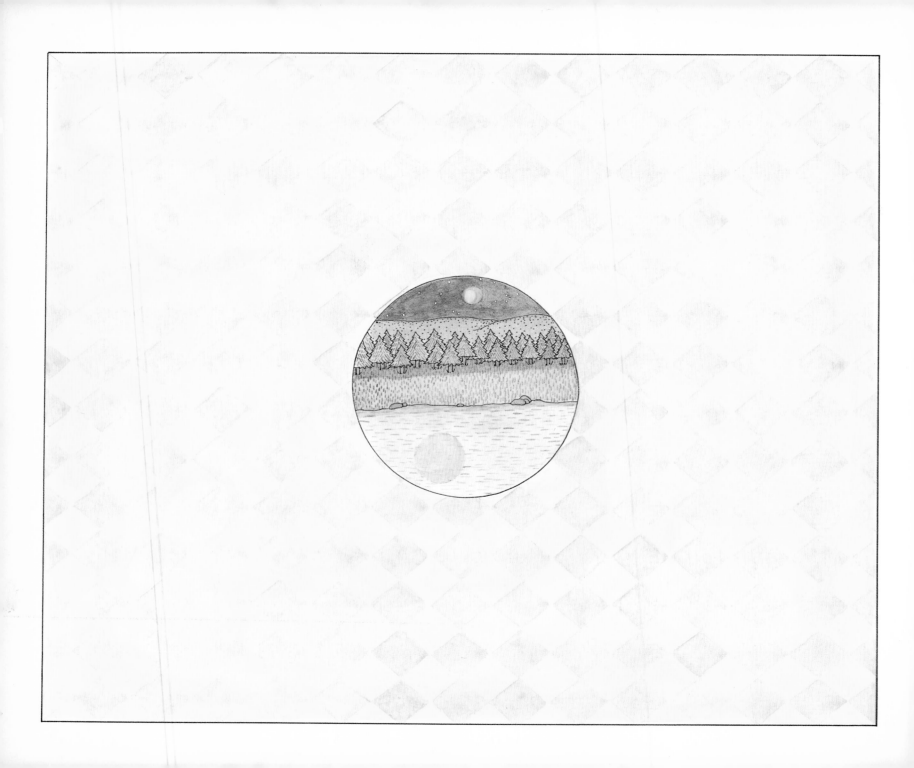